W9-CDK-720

THE BUNYANS

AUDREY WOOD

ILLUSTRATED BY

DAVID SHANNON

THE BLUE SKY PRESS

An Imprint of Scholastic Inc. • New York

For Jennifer and Carl Shaylen
AW

To Sarah and Matthew, and their Aunt Heidi
DS

THE BLUE SKY PRESS

For information regarding permission, please write to: Permissions Department, The Blue Sky Press, an imprint of Scholastic Inc., 555 Broadway, New York, New York 10012.

Special thanks to the Paul Bunyan experts at the Greater Bangor Chamber of Commerce in Maine and the Bemidji Chamber of Commerce in Minnesota.

Library of Congress Cataloging-in-Publication Data
Wood, Audrey. The Bunyans / Audrey Wood; illustrated by David Shannon. p. cm.
Summary: Paul Bunyan, his wife, and their children do some ordinary things which result in the formation of Niagara Falls, Bryce Canyon, and other natural monuments.
ISBN 0-590-48089-8
1. Bunyan, Paul (Legendary character) — Juvenile fiction. [1. Bunyan, Paul (Legendary character) — Fiction. 2. Tall tales. 3. Natural monuments — Fiction. 4. National parks and reserves — Fiction.]
I. Shannon, David, 1959- ill. II. Title.
PZ7.W8468Bu 1996 [E] — dc20 95-26170 CIP AC

12 11 10 9 8 7 6 5 4 3 2 1 6 7 8 9/9 0 1/0

Printed in the United States of America 37
First printing, October 1996

Production supervision by Angela Biola
Designed by Kathleen Westray and David Shannon

STORYTELLER'S NOTE

Now I suppose that you have heard about the mighty logger Paul Bunyan and his great blue ox named Babe. In the early days of our country, Paul and Babe cleared the land for the settlers, so farms and cities could spring up. And you probably know that Paul was taller than a redwood tree, stronger than fifty grizzly bears, and smarter than a library full of books. But you may not know that Paul was married and had two fine children.

ONE DAY WHEN PAUL BUNYAN WAS OUT CLEARING A ROAD THROUGH THE FORESTS of Kentucky, a great pounding began to shake the earth. Looking around, Paul discovered an enormous hole in the side of a hill. The lumberjack pulled up an acre of dry cane and fashioned a torch to light his way.

Paul climbed inside the hole and followed the sound underground for miles, until he came to a large cavern glistening with crystals. By the flickering light of his torch, he saw a gigantic woman banging a behemoth pickax against a wall.

It was love at first sight.

"I'm Carrie McIntie," the gigantic woman said. "I was sitting on the hill when my lucky wishbone fell down a crack into the earth. I've been digging all day trying to find it."

With a grin on his face as wide as the Missouri River, Paul reached into his shirt pocket. "I've got one too," he said, pulling out *his* lucky wishbone. "Marry me, Carrie, and we'll share mine."

Carrie agreed, and their wedding invitations were mailed out right away.

The invitations were so large, only one needed to be sent to each state. Everyone could read them for miles!

The invitations said: *You are cordially invited to the mammoth wedding of Paul Bunyan and Carrie McIntie*. The couple were married in the enormous crystal chamber that Carrie had carved, and after the ceremony, folks began to call it "Mammoth Cave." The giantess had dug more than two hundred miles, making it the longest cave in the world, so the name fit perfectly.

Paul and Carrie settled down on a farm in Maine, and soon there were two new Bunyans. While Pa Bunyan traveled with his logging crew,

Ma Bunyan worked the farm and cared for their jumbo boy, named Little Jean, and their gigantic girl, named Teeny.

One morning when Pa Bunyan was home between jobs, Ma Bunyan cooked up a hearty breakfast of pancakes and syrup. Teeny was wrestling with her big purple puma named Slink and accidentally dumped a silo of syrup on her head. Teeny's hair was so sweet, bears crawled into it and burrowed deep in her curls. Try as they might, Pa and Ma Bunyan couldn't wash them out.

"We'll need a forceful shower of water to get rid of those varmints!" Ma Bunyan declared.

Pa Bunyan had an idea. He placed his daughter on Babe, and he led them to the Niagara River in Canada. The gargantuan father scooped out a huge hole in the middle of the riverbed. As the great river roared down into the deep hole, Teeny cried out in delight, "Niagara falls!" Teeny showered in the waterfall, and the pesky bears were washed downstream.

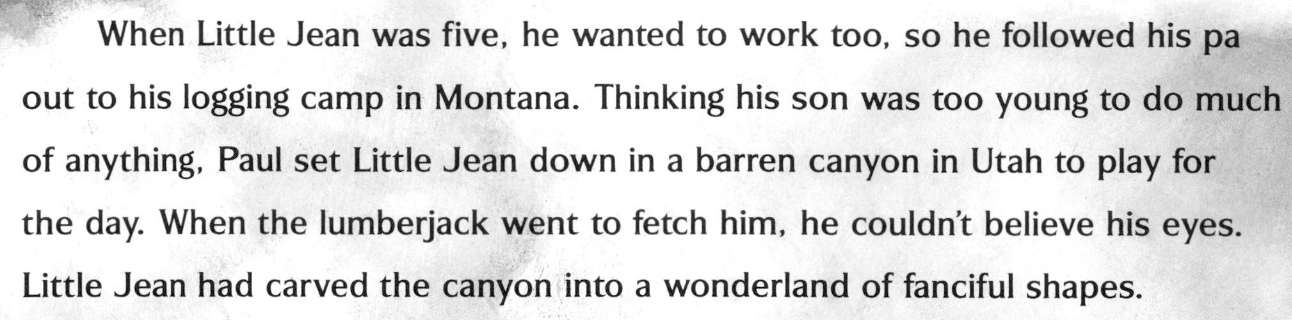

When Little Jean was five, he wanted to work too, so he followed his pa out to his logging camp in Montana. Thinking his son was too young to do much of anything, Paul set Little Jean down in a barren canyon in Utah to play for the day. When the lumberjack went to fetch him, he couldn't believe his eyes. Little Jean had carved the canyon into a wonderland of fanciful shapes.

Pa Bunyan got tongue-tied and said, "That's a mighty *brice* nanyon, coy, I mean, a mighty nice canyon, boy!" Somehow part of the mix-up stuck.

To this day the canyon is known as Bryce Canyon.

After all that sculpting, Little Jean's shoes were full of sand. Pa knew Ma Bunyan wouldn't want her clean floors dirtied up, so he told Little Jean to sit down and empty out his shoes.

The sand from Little Jean's shoes blew away on the eastern wind and settled down a state away. It covered a valley ten miles long, making sand dunes eight hundred feet high. Everyone knows that's how the Great Sand Dunes of Colorado came to be.

One summer, Little Jean and Teeny wanted to go to the beach. Ma Bunyan told them to follow a river to the ocean. But all the rivers flowed west back then, so they missed the Atlantic Ocean and ended up on the other side of the country instead.

Ma Bunyan tracked them out to the Pacific Ocean, where she

found Teeny riding on the backs of two blue whales and Little Jean carving out fifty zigzag miles of the California coast.

When Ma Bunyan saw what her son had done, she exclaimed, "What's the big idea, sir!?" From that time on, the scenic area was known as Big Sur.

Ma Bunyan knew she had to put up a barrier to remind her children not to wander off too far. So, on the way home, everyone pitched in and built the Rocky Mountains. Teeny gathered up and sorted out all the rivers, letting some flow east and others west. After that, the children had no trouble following the eastern rivers down to the Atlantic Ocean. And when they wanted to go out exploring, Ma Bunyan would call out, "Now don't cross the Continental Divide, children!"

The best thing about camping is sleeping outdoors, and the worst thing is not having enough hot water. That's why the Bunyans always camped in Wyoming. By the time their camping years were over, Ma Bunyan had poked more than three hundred holes in the ground with her pickax and released tons of hot water from geysers. But Ma got tired of poking so many holes, so she made a geyser that blew every hour on the hour. After that, there was a steady supply of hot water to keep the giants' clothes and dishes sparkling clean.

Teeny named the geyser Old Faithful, and to this day, Old Faithful still blows its top every hour in Yellowstone National Park.

As our great country grew up, so did the Bunyan children. When the kids left home, Ma and Pa Bunyan retired to a wilderness area, where they still live happily.

Teeny hitched a ride on a whale over to England and became a famous fashion designer. Her colorful skirts made from air balloons and her breezy blouses cut from ship sails were a sensation at the first World's Fair in London.

Little Jean traveled to Venice, Italy, where he studied astronomy and art. Every day, the gondoliers would take their passengers down the Grand Canal to watch the giant artist chiseling his marble sculptures.

After graduation, Little Jean decided to explore new lands, as his parents had done. So he took two great jumps and one flying leap and bounded up into outer space.

In 1976, the year of our country's bicentennial, a spacecraft sent by the National Aeronautics and Space Administration was on a mission to study Mars. The spacecraft was named *Viking I*, and it took many photographs of the surface of the planet. One mysterious photo looked like a face carved out of colossal rock.

Some say the photograph is not a face, but an illusion caused by light and shadows on the rock. Others think the famous "Martian face" is just the spitting image of Little Jean Bunyan. If that's so, who knows what he's up to on the other planets.

Only time will tell!